Transformers Annual 2010
First published in Great Britain by HarperCollins Children's Books in 2009.

When Robots Attack adapted by Ray Santos. Illustrated by MADA Design, Inc. Digital colours by Kanila
Tripp. Based on the Screenplay by Ehren Kruger & Alex Kurtzman & Roberto Orci. Operation Autobot
adapted by Susan Korman. Illustrated by MADA Design, Inc. Based on the Screenplay by Ehren Kruger &
Alex Kurtzman & Roberto Orci.

13 5 7 9 10 8 6 4 2
ISBN-13: 978-0-00-731087-6

Printed and bound in China.

TRANSFORMERS
REVENGE OF THE FALLEN

ANNUAL 2010

HarperCollins *Children's Books*

Contents

Return of the Robots

When Sam Witwicky got his first car – a beaten-up, yellow Camaro with black racing stripes – the last thing he expected was for it to turn into alien robot Bumblebee! The car changed his life, but not in the way he was expecting...

Bumblebee is one of a team of Autobots - Transformers from the planet Cybertron – that came to Earth to search for the AllSpark, the life force of the Transformers. The evil leader of the Decepticons, Megatron, sought the power of the AllSpark and had destroyed Cybertron in a fight to gain control of it. He intended to use it to defeat the Autobots and conquer the universe. A great war raged between the Autobots and the Decepticons, but the AllSpark was lost, falling into space until it landed on Earth. Megatron fell too, and was trapped in the Arctic ice for many years.

A crew of explorers, led by Sam's grandfather, Captain Archibald Witwicky, stumbled upon the frozen Decepticon. Megatron used the last of his energy to imprint a map with the location of the AllSpark on to Archibald's glasses.

Many years later, Sam discovered that Bumblebee was sent by the Autobots to protect him and his grandfather's glasses. And Bumblebee was not alone. Two factions of Transformers came to Earth: the Decepticons to find their leader and the AllSpark, and the Autobots to protect Earth and prevent the Decepticons from gaining the power they desired.

Sam and his new friend, Mikaela, helped the Autobots track down the AllSpark to the Hoover Dam, but the Decepticons were already on their way. The two teenagers found themselves caught up in an ancient battle for the source of all Cybertronian power, which climaxed with a fight between the Autobot and Decepticon leaders, Optimus Prime and Megatron. Sam went to Prime's aid and used the power of the AllSpark to destroy Megatron. His body was dumped in the deep seas of the Laurentian Abyss, never to be seen again...

Until now.

A new team of Decepticons have landed on a distant planet in the spaceship Nemesis. Led by Starscream, a survivor of the earlier battle, they again seek control of the power of the AllSpark. Megatron is revived and answers to an ancient evil, The Fallen, who long ago created a machine capable of taking the sun's energy and destroying the planet. The Fallen has risen again and intends to return to activate his machine.

Only with Sam's help can the Autobots stop the Decepticons from putting their plans into action. But Sam's at college now and just wants a normal life. Will he face up to his fate and help his friends? Is there more to Sam than meets the eye?

Locations in Disguise

Find all the places that appear in *Revenge of the Fallen* in the grid below.
They can appear horizontally, vertically, diagonally and even backwards.

California

New York City

Diego Garcia Air Base

Pentagon

Egypt

University

Nemesis

Washington DC

```
F G W E R Y I P L J G D A Z C B M L O
T R S F G E T G Y H N M J I O L Q A Z
D I E G O G A R C I A A I R B A S E C
B N N F A Y Z C B M K H F S Q O H N E
I C E L H P A C A L I F O R N I A L L
Y L V M B T E D G T H U Y D S A N V X
B T N T E S A E W C V T P N Y F G H J
A D S D F S A E R T Y J E O A N H N A
W N H O K G I Y T I U H N S D W A B N
P U O I N Y T S V B Y E T G R W I B I
L N P Q S C V G Y U W K A M L P O J B
H I U Y T R F F D Y S X G V B N U T F
I V J O O H N P O E B T O G I J I B K
Z E A Q W S X R C D E R N F V B G T Y
H R N M J Y K U K I O L P M N B V V C
X S Z A D C S F G J H I K O U Y T R E
W I Q G I F R D S H N B V I U Y T G D
I T B T X W A S H I N G T O N D C L I
H Y Y M I U N Y H O F F R E S P J Y N
```

Colour Devastator

Lots of different construction vehicles combine to make the monstrous Devastator.

Transformer Sightings 2009

Laurentian Abyss, North Atlantic Ocean

Enemy leader, classified NBE-I rusting with military surveillance.

Sam's University, New Jersey

Sam Witwicky, friend of the Autobots, is attending college here. Decepticon sighted disguised as student.

Smithsonian Institute, Washington, D.C.

Ancient Decepticon known as Jetfire, also revealed to have defected to the Autobots.

California

Small Decepticon known as Wheels captured by Mikaela Banes. Has defected to the side of the Autobots.

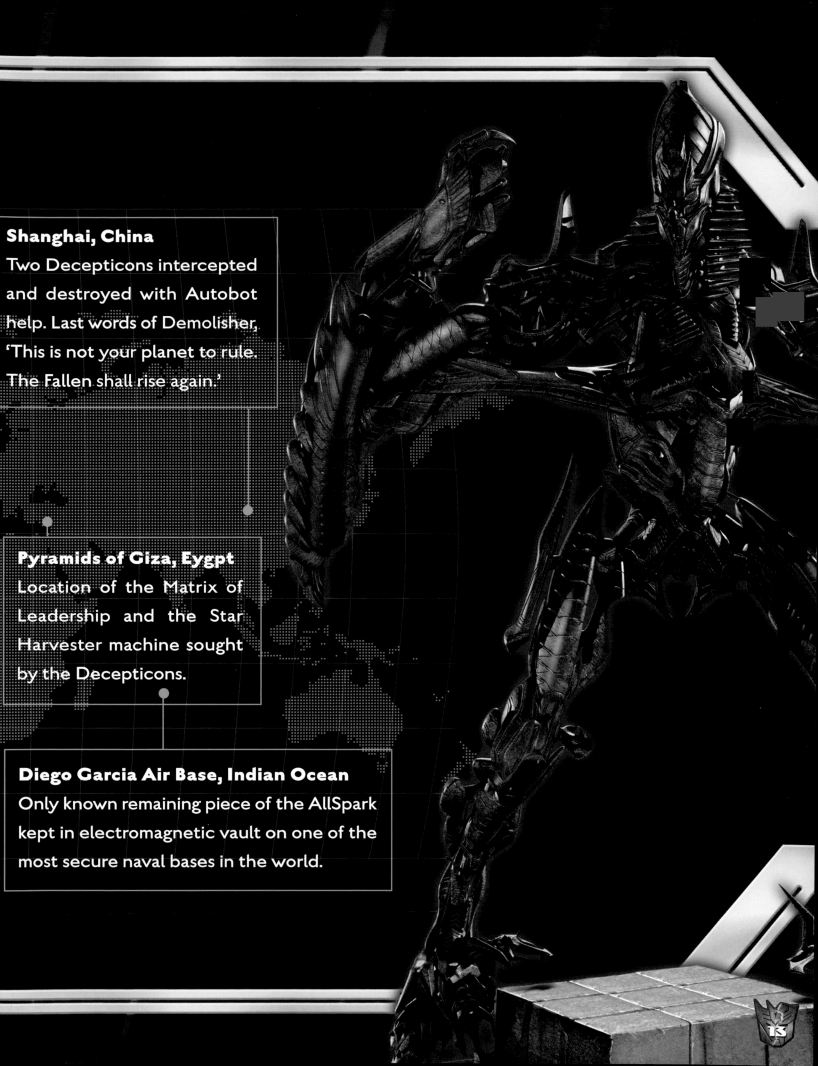

Shanghai, China
Two Decepticons intercepted and destroyed with Autobot help. Last words of Demolisher, 'This is not your planet to rule. The Fallen shall rise again.'

Pyramids of Giza, Eygpt
Location of the Matrix of Leadership and the Star Harvester machine sought by the Decepticons.

Diego Garcia Air Base, Indian Ocean
Only known remaining piece of the AllSpark kept in electromagnetic vault on one of the most secure naval bases in the world.

Spot the Difference

There are seven differences between these two pictures of
Skids and Mudflap. How many can you find?

Save the Sun

Scale the pyramid and prevent the Decepticons from activating the sun harvester machine.

END

START

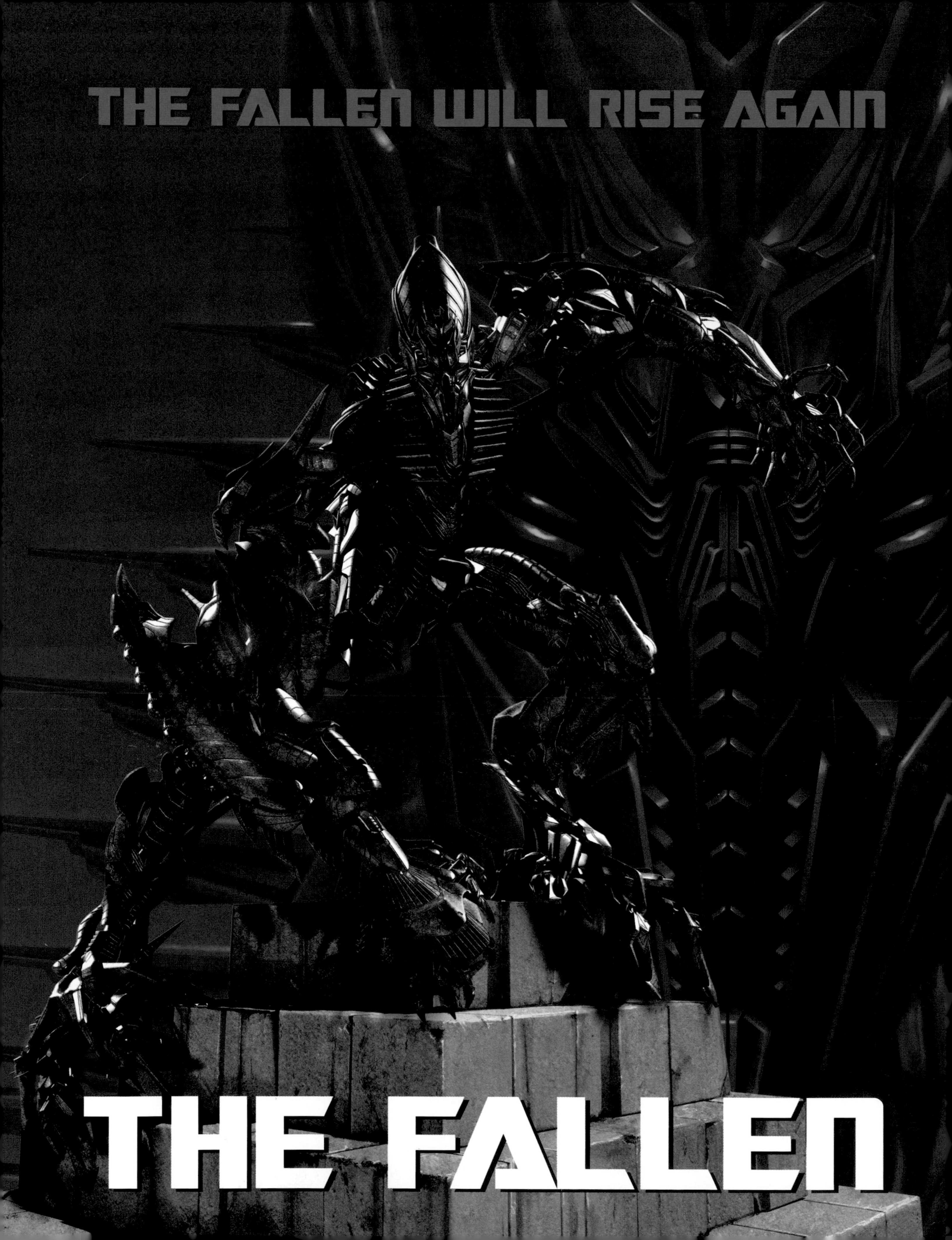

THE FALLEN WILL RISE AGAIN

THE FALLEN

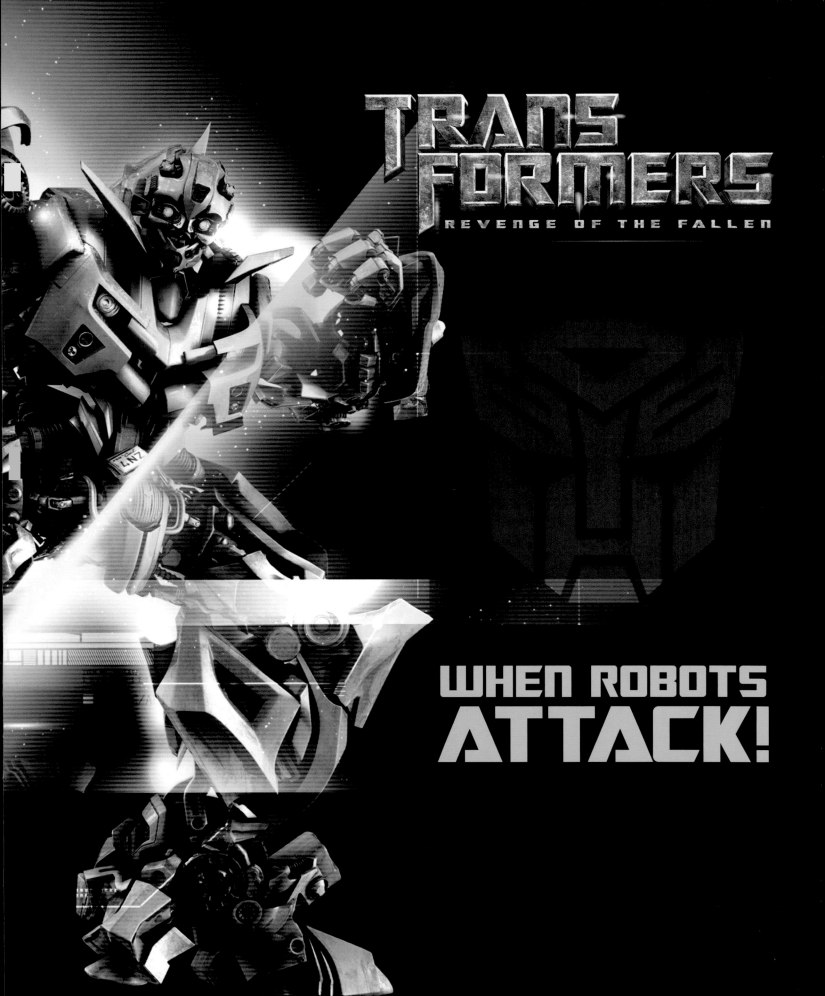

Two years ago, Sam Witwicky's life changed forever when his first car turned into a giant robot named Bumblebee. He was part of an alien race called Transformers, who had come to Earth looking for the AllSpark.

The AllSpark cube was the source of the alien life and could create Transformers from regular mechanical objects.

The evil Decepticons tried to use the AllSpark to rule the Earth, but Sam and his friends the Autobots fought back.

Sam smashed the AllSpark into the Decepticon leader's chest, destroying both.

Things eventually returned to normal for Sam – if having a Transformer for a car was normal! Now Sam was packing for his next adventure: college.

"Look what I found!" said Sam's mum. "Your baby booties!"
"We're both really proud of you, kiddo," said his dad. "You're the first Witwicky to go to college!"
Sam groaned and handed his dad a box to put in the car.

Up in his room, Sam sorted through a pile of clothes. He found the shirt he was wearing the day he had saved the world by destroying the AllSpark.

Or at least he thought the AllSpark had been destroyed. When Sam held up the shirt, a tiny sliver fell out of the pocket!

Sam tried to catch the piece of AllSpark, but its powerful energy gave him a shock. Sam dropped the sliver on the floor, and it quickly burned a hole all the way down to the kitchen. The electric outlets in the walls began to spark.

Sam's touch had activated the AllSpark, and Sam knew that even a small piece had enough power to create an army of evil robots. He had to destroy it!

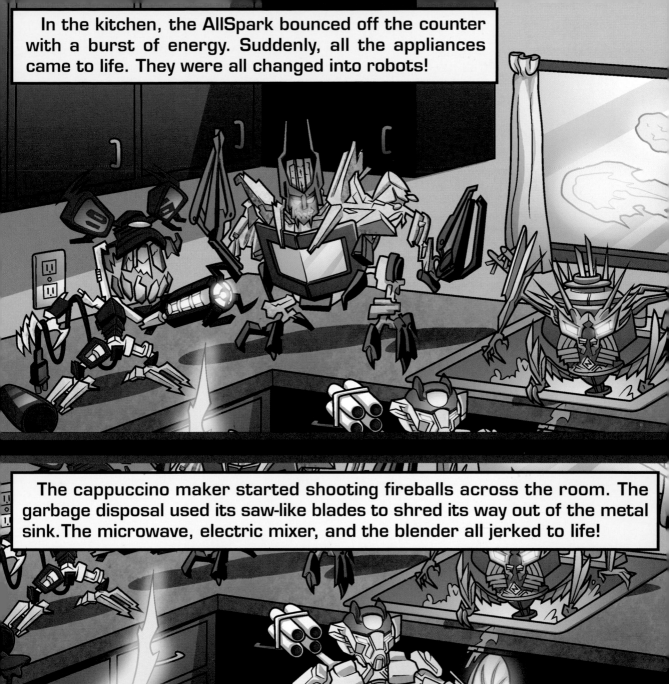

In the kitchen, the AllSpark bounced off the counter with a burst of energy. Suddenly, all the appliances came to life. They were all changed into robots!

The cappuccino maker started shooting fireballs across the room. The garbage disposal used its saw-like blades to shred its way out of the metal sink. The microwave, electric mixer, and the blender all jerked to life!

In Sam's room, the sparking outlets had started a fire. He poured a bottle of water over the flames, but water doesn't put out electrical fires. It just drained through the hole in the floor!

In the kitchen, the blender noticed the water dripping down from the ceiling. Water could short out the small robots! The blender ordered the other 'bots to march upstairs and find the source. The cappuccino maker left a trail of coffee on the floor.

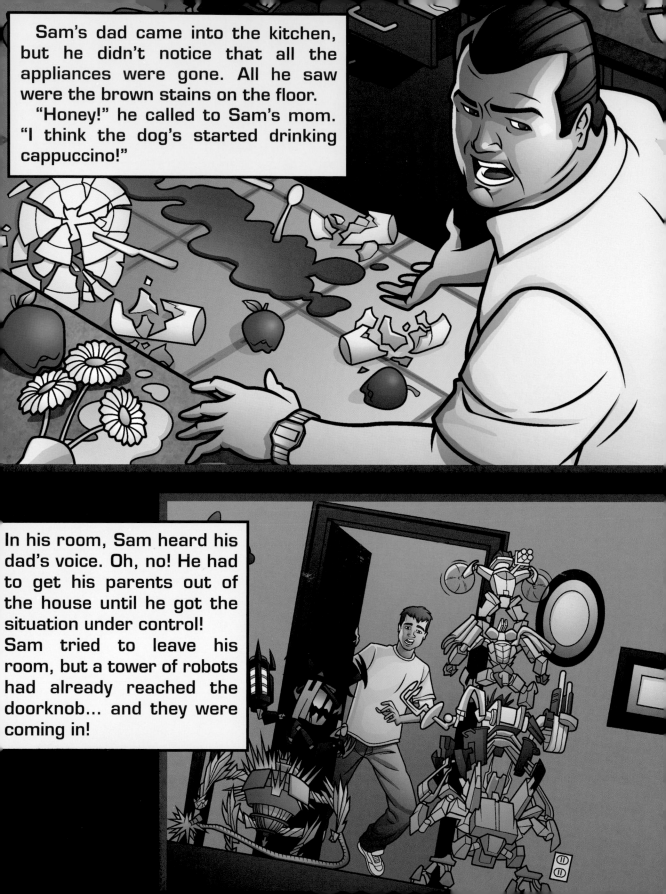

Sam's dad came into the kitchen, but he didn't notice that all the appliances were gone. All he saw were the brown stains on the floor.

"Honey!" he called to Sam's mom. "I think the dog's started drinking cappuccino!"

In his room, Sam heard his dad's voice. Oh, no! He had to get his parents out of the house until he got the situation under control! Sam tried to leave his room, but a tower of robots had already reached the doorknob... and they were coming in!

The appliances swarmed into the room. All of them had parts that had changed into horrible weapons. An egg beater hit Sam in the knees, and then the mixer started firing. Metal pellets hit the fish tank. Water splashed everywhere!

Sam hid behind his desk and looked around, but the only way to escape was through the window.

Sam climbed out of the window and tumbled to the ground. Luckily, there were some bushes to break his fall.

As Sam landed with a loud thud, his dad came out into the backyard.

"What's all the racket?" he yelled.

The electric mixer bot looked out the bedroom window. Its arms turned into rocket launchers and started firing missiles.

"Dad! Take cover!" Sam called as the doghouse behind them exploded.

Sam's mum came running from the house with a waffle iron chasing her. "AAAAH!" she screamed. The evil robots were going to hurt his parents! Sam needed help.

"BUMBLEBEE!" yelled Sam. The yellow car with black racing stripes crashed through the wall of their garage and screeched to a stop in front of Sam.

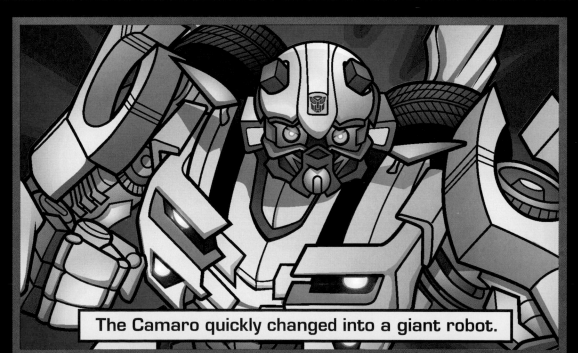

The Camaro quickly changed into a giant robot.

The small home appliances were no match for Bumblebee. He was able to destroy the renegade robots with a few quick blasts from his plasma cannon.

The only problem was that Bumblebee also completely destroyed Sam's house!

Sam was relieved that the battle was over, but his mum was very upset. She turned to Bumblebee and yelled, "My house! I want that talking alien car out of here!"

Bumblebee knew that he was in trouble, but he didn't mind. He had done his job protecting Sam, and the family was safe again!

THE END

The History of the Primes

All the recorded history of the Transformers was lost when the AllSpark was destroyed, but some of its knowledge lives on in Sam. When he touched a charred ember that remained from the AllSpark, his mind was flooded with alien symbols – the language of the Primes. The symbols are the story of the genesis of the Transformer race.

The AllSpark created thirteen Transformers to bring life to the planet Cybertron. They were the first of their kind and known as the Dynasty of the Primes. Together they governed over the other Transformers. The AllSpark also created the Matrix of Leadership. Its power could be used to activate a machine built to destroy suns and collect their energy. One of the Primes, the Fallen, wanted all its power to himself. He gradually killed all the Primes until only he and one other remained. The other Prime was mortally wounded and built a wall around the Matrix and the bodies of the eleven dead Primes. He sealed the tomb with his own body, sacrificing himself to save the Matrix. The Star Harvester fell to Earth and was buried beneath the desert sands. The Egyptians built a pyramid over it and it remained hidden for many years.

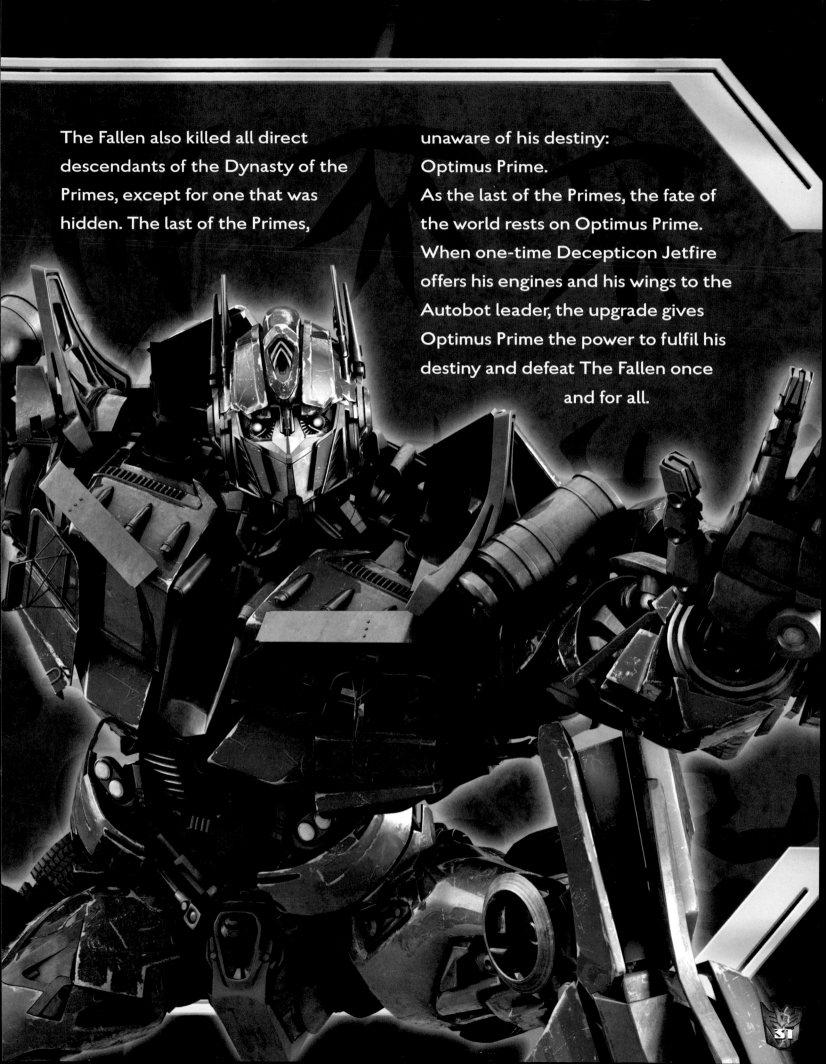

The Fallen also killed all direct descendants of the Dynasty of the Primes, except for one that was hidden. The last of the Primes, unaware of his destiny: Optimus Prime.

As the last of the Primes, the fate of the world rests on Optimus Prime. When one-time Decepticon Jetfire offers his engines and his wings to the Autobot leader, the upgrade gives Optimus Prime the power to fulfil his destiny and defeat The Fallen once and for all.

Battle for the Pyramid

You will need:
At least two players
A counter or coin for each player
A die

How to play:
The youngest player goes first. Take turns rolling the die and moving the number of spaces shown around the pyramid. Follow the instructions if you land on any. The winner is the first player to make it to the top of the pyramid.

Receive
an upgrad
fly forwar
two block

Dodge
Megatron's fire –
run forwards two
blocks.

START

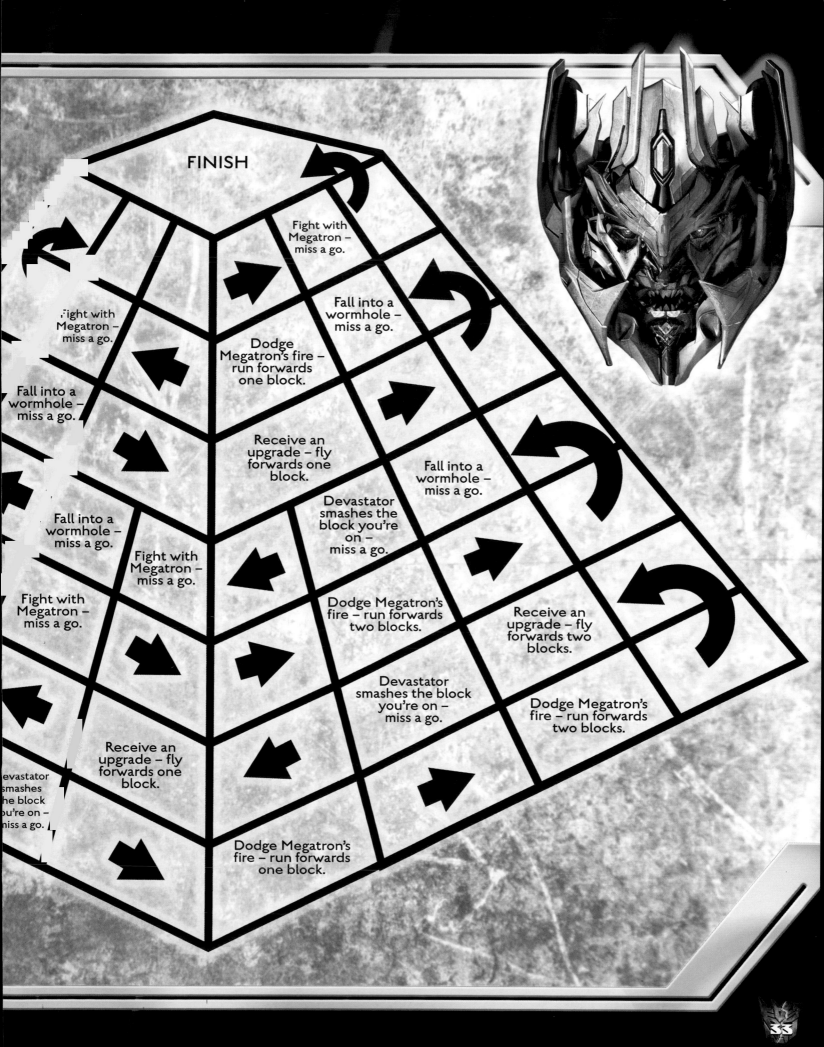

FINISH

Fight with Megatron – miss a go.

Fall into a wormhole – miss a go.

Fight with Megatron – miss a go.

Dodge Megatron's fire – run forwards one block.

Fall into a wormhole – miss a go.

Receive an upgrade – fly forwards one block.

Fall into a wormhole – miss a go.

Devastator smashes the block you're on – miss a go.

Fall into a wormhole – miss a go.

Fight with Megatron – miss a go.

Fight with Megatron – miss a go.

Dodge Megatron's fire – run forwards two blocks.

Receive an upgrade – fly forwards two blocks.

Devastator smashes the block you're on – miss a go.

Dodge Megatron's fire – run forwards two blocks.

Devastator smashes the block you're on – miss a go.

Receive an upgrade – fly forwards one block.

Dodge Megatron's fire – run forwards one block.

Whose Side Are You On?

If you had to take sides and team up with the Transformers, would you make a better Autobot or Decepticon? Choose a starting point for the test below and see which Transformer you are most like.

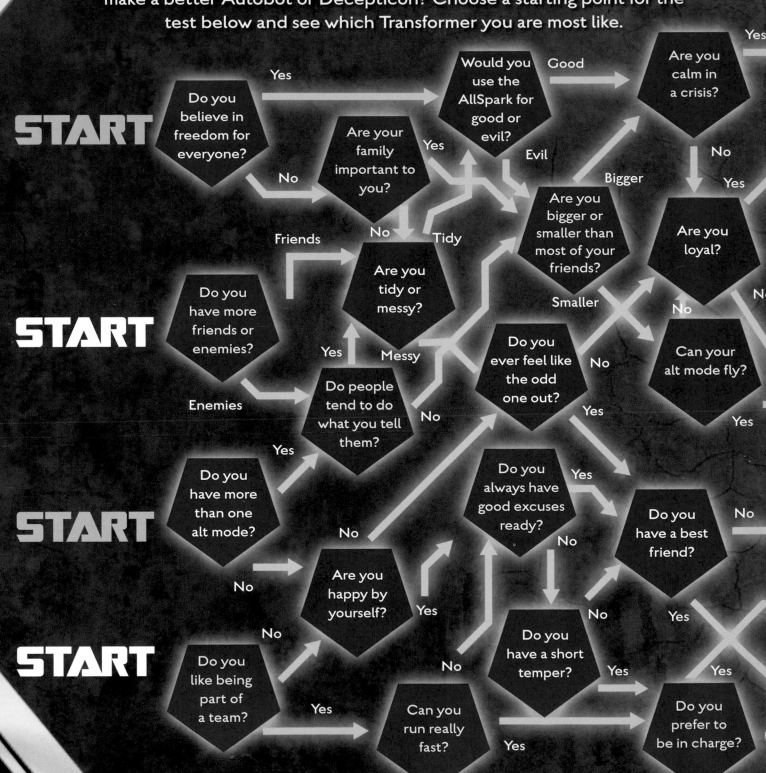

START — Do you believe in freedom for everyone? — Yes → Would you use the AllSpark for good or evil? — Good → Are you calm in a crisis? — Yes / No

No → Are your family important to you? — Yes → / No → Are you tidy or messy? — Tidy / Messy

Would you use the AllSpark for good or evil? — Evil → Are you bigger or smaller than most of your friends? — Bigger → Are you loyal? / Smaller

Are you calm in a crisis? — No → Are you loyal? — No → Can your alt mode fly? — Yes

START — Do you have more friends or enemies? — Friends → Are you tidy or messy? — Messy → Do you ever feel like the odd one out? — Yes / No

Enemies → Do people tend to do what you tell them? — Yes → / No →

Are you bigger or smaller than most of your friends? — Smaller → Can your alt mode fly? — No

Do you ever feel like the odd one out? — No → Do you always have good excuses ready? — Yes / No → Do you have a best friend?

START — Do you have more than one alt mode? — Yes → Do people tend to do what you tell them? / No → Are you happy by yourself? — Yes / No

Do you always have good excuses ready? — No → Do you have a short temper? — Yes / No

Do you have a best friend? — No / Yes

START — Do you like being part of a team? — No → Are you happy by yourself? — Yes / Yes → Can you run really fast? — Yes → Do you have a short temper? — Yes → Do you prefer to be in charge? — Yes / Yes

Do you stand by your friends, no matter what? — Yes →

Optimus Prime
You are most like Optimus Prime. You make a fair leader and your friends can always depend on you. You are calm and good-hearted.

No

Do you like humans? — No

Yes

Megatron
You are most like Megatron. You are single-minded about your goals and won't let anyone get in your way. Try not to be such a bully!

Yes

Are you superior to everyone else? — No

Wheels
You are most like Wheels. You are adaptable and stand up for what you believe in, even if it means disagreeing with your friends.

Yes

Have you ever swapped teams?

No

Starscream
You are most like Starscream. You hate being bossed around and want to be in control of your own destiny.

No

Do you question authority? — Yes

No

Do you sometimes talk in song lyrics? — Yes →

Bumblebee
You are most like Bumblebee. You're fun to have around and a great team player. You like to take care of your friends and are always ready for anything.

Colour The Fallen

One of the Original Primes, The Fallen, has risen again to destroy Earth.

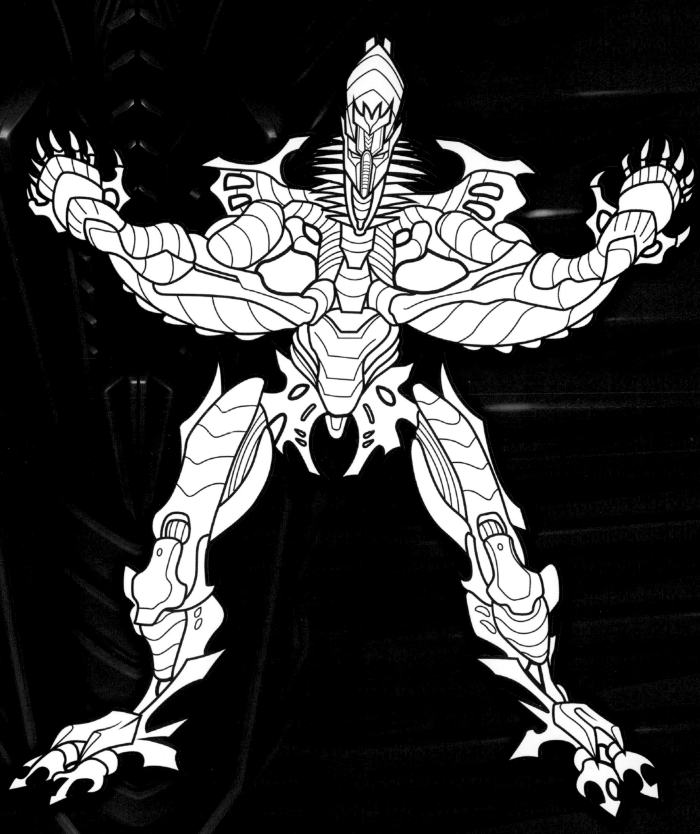

TRANSFORMERS
REVENGE OF THE FALLEN

OPERATION AUTOBOT

Screech! Military vehicles squealed to a stop. A team of soldiers roped off an area for a top secret operation. They were tracking down dangerous aliens named Decepticons!

Soldiers leaped from the back of a pick-up truck. The truck switched into the powerful Autobot Ironhide! Suddenly, the Tracker blipped furiously. The enemies were close!

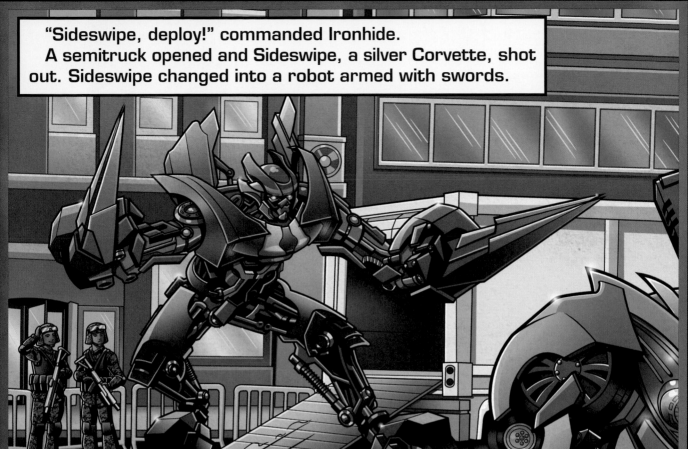

"Sideswipe, deploy!" commanded Ironhide.
A semitruck opened and Sideswipe, a silver Corvette, shot out. Sideswipe changed into a robot armed with swords.

The Twins arrived to help. "You just try to stay out of trouble, okay?" Ironhide told the mischievous robots.

The team tracked the signal to a construction vehicle parked near some cement pipes.

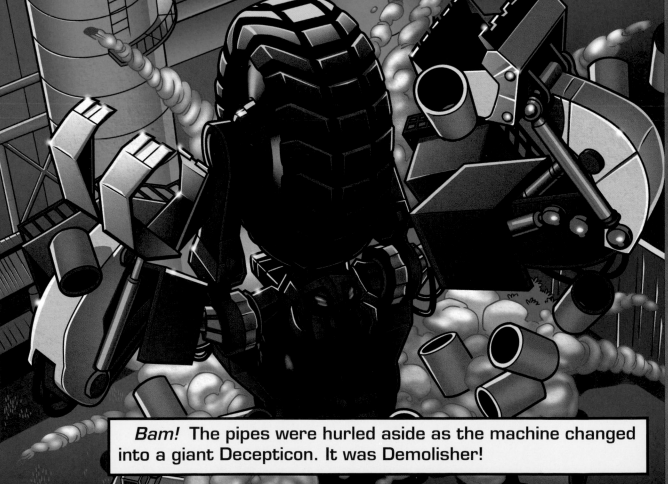

Bam! The pipes were hurled aside as the machine changed into a giant Decepticon. It was Demolisher!

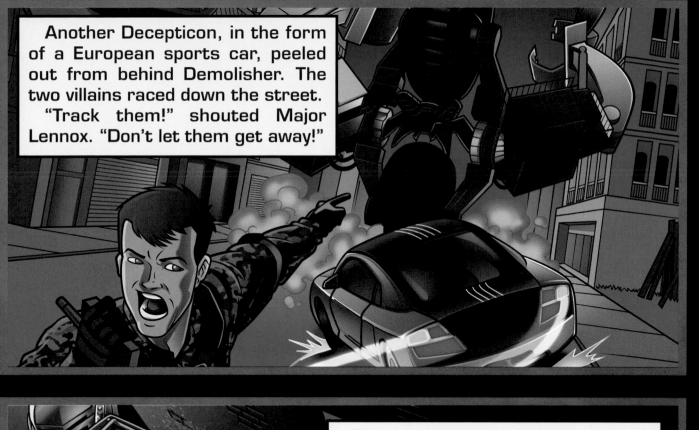

Another Decepticon, in the form of a European sports car, peeled out from behind Demolisher. The two villains raced down the street. "Track them!" shouted Major Lennox. "Don't let them get away!"

The sports car ripped through narrow alleyways. The Twins tried to follow, but the space was too tight!

The Decepticon switched into his robot form, bursting through a brick wall!

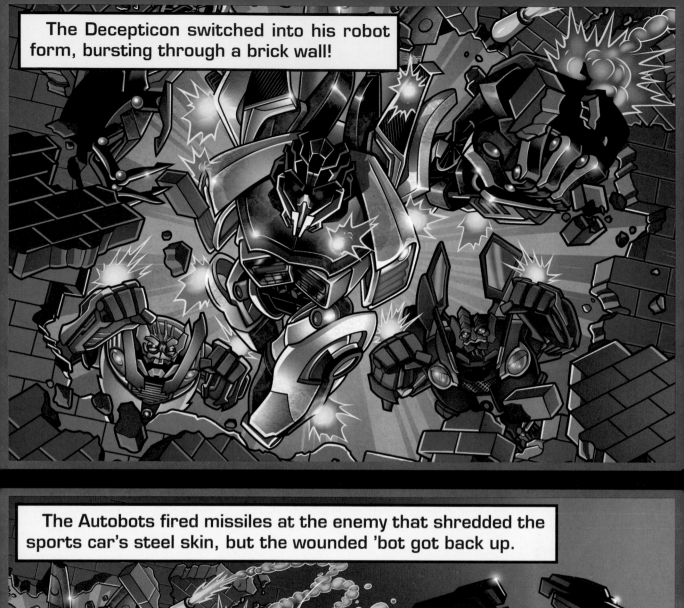

The Autobots fired missiles at the enemy that shredded the sports car's steel skin, but the wounded 'bot got back up.

Suddenly, Sideswipe roared up to the scene. He used his swords to slash at the 'bot.

The Decepticon fought back, sending a powerful energy pulse across the ground. The blast rippled down the street, rushing toward Sideswipe!

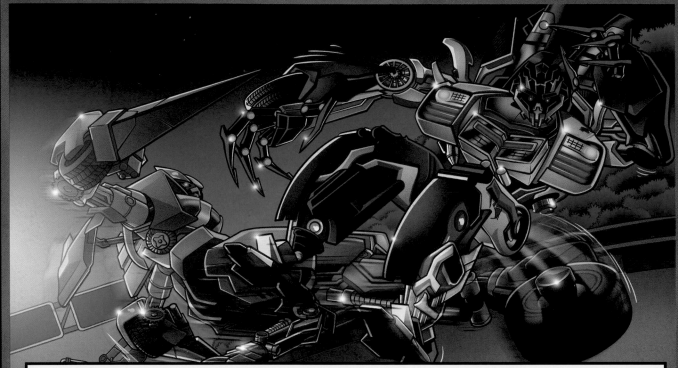

Sideswipe sprang out of the way just in time and advanced toward the Decepticon. With one swift motion, Sideswipe flipped the Decepticon's legs into the air, stopping it for good.

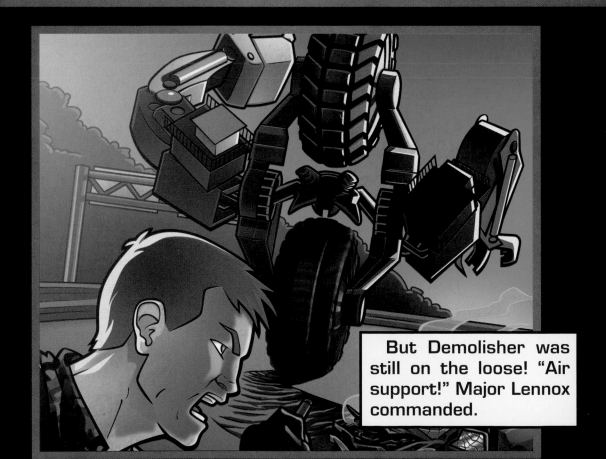

But Demolisher was still on the loose! "Air support!" Major Lennox commanded.

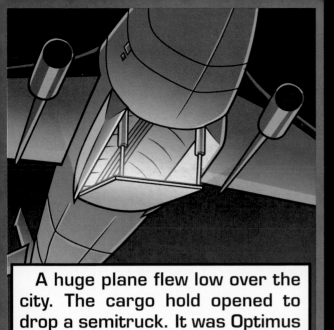

A huge plane flew low over the city. The cargo hold opened to drop a semitruck. It was Optimus Prime – the commander of the Autobots!

Optimus sped after the massive Decepticon. Demolisher stood on one wheel, flipping end-over-end. As he rolled along, he crushed cars and everything else in his path!

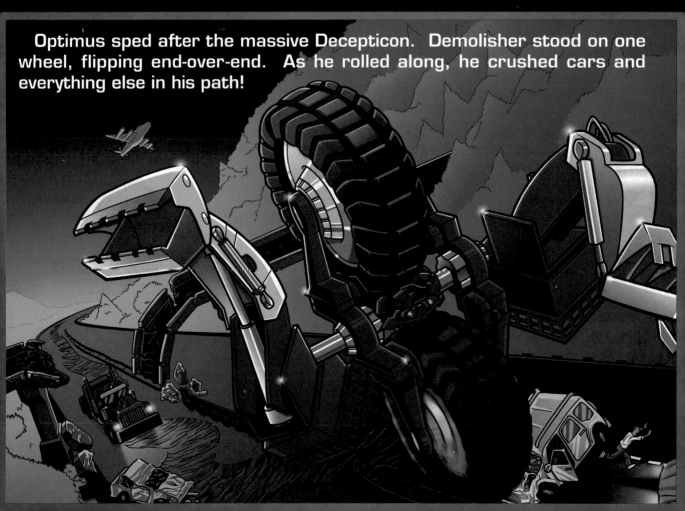

Optimus switched into robot mode, jumping on to Demolisher's back!

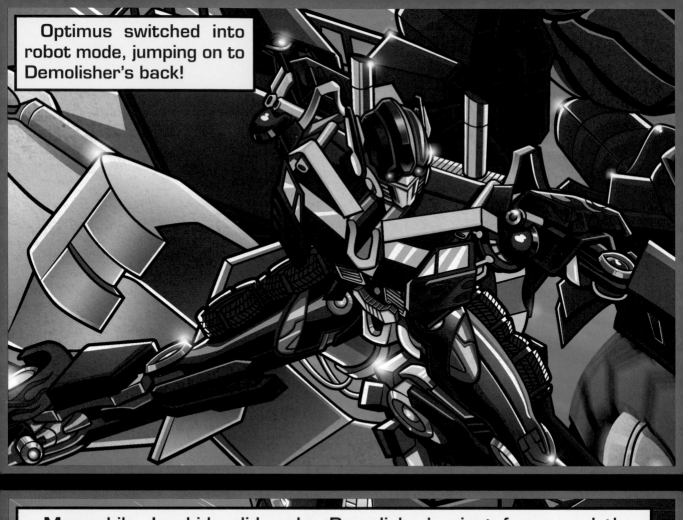

Meanwhile, Ironhide slid under Demolisher's giant frame and then swung on to one of his wheels. Together he and Optimus slammed into the Decepticon from both sides.

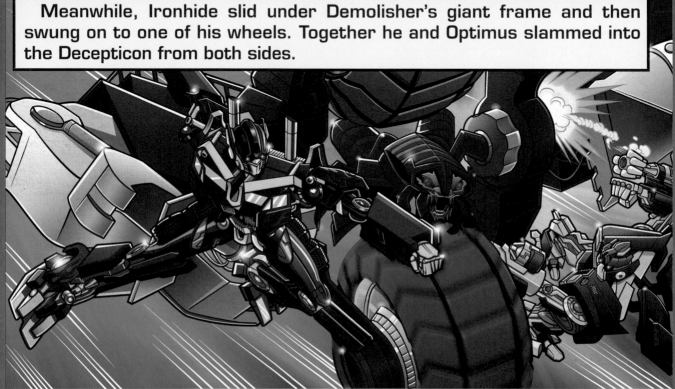

Finally, Demolisher wobbled to a halt. Optimus stood over his captured enemy. "Leave Earth alone," the Autobot ordered.

"This is not your planet to rule . . ." Demolisher warned him, gasping for breath. "The Fallen shall rise again. . . ."

For now, the Autobots and their friends had stopped the savage Decepticons. But they knew they had to be ready. There was a bigger battle on the horizon.

THE END

Transform and Roll Out!

All the Transformers, Autobot or Decepticon, have cool alt-modes.
Match these Transformers to the vehicles they can change into.

A   B   C   D

1

2

3

4

Shadow Match

Match each of the charcters below to their correct silhouette.

A

B

C

1

2

3

D

4

5

E

6

F

G

7

H

8

Colour Megatron

Megatron is finally free to try and capture the Allspark.

Code of the Primes

Jetfire is having trouble reading the language of the Primes. Help him work out what this message says.

A D E G H I K L N O

P R S T V W Y

WHEN DAWN ALIGHTS
the DAGGER'S TIP,
ThREE KINGS WILL
REVEAL the DOORWAY.

Transformer Tracker

Which of the Transformers is below Ratchet, above Skids and between Optimus Prime and Sideswipe? Circle the answer.

Bumblebee

YOUR NEW BEST FRIEND

ALLSpark Grid

Cross out every instance of the word 'AllSpark' in this grid to
reveal what Sam needs to save Optimus Prime.

M A L L S P A R K A
T R A L L S P A R K
A L L S P A R K I X
O A L L S P A R K F
L E A L L S P A R K
A L L S P A R K A D
E A L L S P A R K R
S H A L L S P A R K
A L L S P A R K I P

Memory Machine

Take a good long look at this picture, then turn the page
and see what you can remember.

Questions

1. What are the names of the charcters in the picure on Page 57?

2. Who is on the left?

3. What colour is the picture background?

4. Who is on the right?

5. How many Autobots are in the picture?

Answers

Page 10
Locations in Disguise

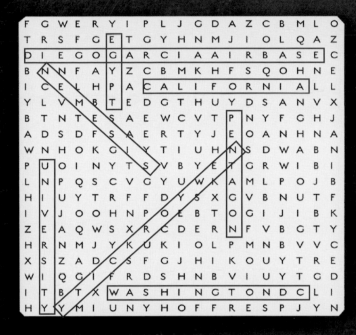

Page 14
Spot the Difference

Page 15
Save the Sun

Page 49
Transform and Roll Out

A=3=Bumblebee, B=1=Megatron, C=2=Optimus Prime, D=4=Ratchet

Page 50
Shadow Match

A=6=Magatron, B=7= Starscream, C=5= Ironhide, D=4= Devastator, E=8=Ratchet, F=2=Sideswipe, G=1=The Fallen, H=3=Skids

Page 53
Code of the Primes

The code reads 'When dawn alights the dagger's tip, Three Kings will reveal the doorway.'

Page 54
Transformer Tracker

Mudflap.

Page 56
AllSpark Grid

Sam needs the Matrix of Leadership.

Page 58
Memory Machine: Questions.

1. The Fallen, Sideswipe, Megatron and Devastator.
2. The Fallen 3. Black 4. Megatron 5. One